Flying Feet

A Mud Flat Story

JAMES STEVENSON

Greenwillow Books
An Imprint of HarperCollins*Publishers*

Flying Feet: A Mud Flat Story
Copyright © 2004 by James Stevenson
Manufactured in China
by South China Printing Company Ltd.
www.harperchildrens.com

Watercolor paints and a black pen
were used to prepare the full-color art.
The text type is Symbol ITC Medium.

Library of Congress
Cataloging-in-Publication Data

Stevenson, James.
Flying Feet: A Mud Flat Story /
by James Stevenson.
  p. cm.
"Greenwillow Books."
Summary: Stan and the other animals
of Mud Flat take dance lessons from
some touring tap dancers and prepare
for a big show.
ISBN 0-06-051975-4 (trade)
ISBN 0-06-051976-2 (lib. bdg.)
[1. Dance—Fiction.
2. Tap dancing—Fiction.
3. Animals—Fiction.] I. Title.
PZ7.S84748 Fn 2004 [E]—dc21
                    2002029785

First Edition
10 9 8 7 6 5 4 3 2 1

Greenwillow Books

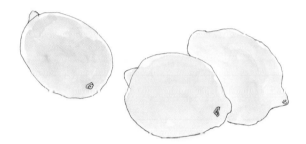

For Naomi,
with love

Contents

.1.
STRANGE NOISE

"What a lovely day in Mud Flat," said Maureen,
sniffing the air. "I believe the skunk cabbage
is coming into bloom."

"Great," said Stan.

"And the beach plums are blossoming,"
said Maureen. "Gorgeous."

"All I want to do is get out of here," said Stan,
    tossing his baseball.

"What in the world for?" said Maureen.
"I want to be a famous star, like a baseball
    player," said Stan. "I want crowds of people
    to clap and cheer for me."
"That would be nice," said Maureen.
"What's that noise?" said Stan.

"It sounds like a bunch of giant woodpeckers,"
said Maureen.
"Let's go see!" said Stan.

There was a big crowd in front of the post office.

Stan climbed on top of Neddy to get
a better view.

"Oh, wow!" said Stan.

Two dancers in fancy clothes were tap-dancing on
the back of a van. Their feet moved so fast that
Stan could hardly see them.

The crowd clapped.

"Thank you, ladies and gentlemen!" said the man.

"We are the famous dance team of Tonya and Ted!"

"Here's a little sample
of our sensational steps,"
said Ted.

RAT-TA TATA

HOP-HIP-HIPPITY-HOP-HOP

SHUFFA
DA SHUFFA

"We are here to offer you tap-dancing lessons
at a special low price!"
said Tonya.
"Once you learn,"
said Ted,
"you will dance
in Tonya and Ted's
fabulous
Flying Feet show!"

"I want to do that!"
said Stan.
"Form a line over here, folks,"
said Ted,
"and have your money with you."

Stan ran home as fast
as he could.

He got the tin box from under his bed and
took out most of the money he had saved
for a baseball glove.

Then he ran back and
gave the money to Ted.

"Where are your tap shoes?"
said Ted.
"I don't have any," said Stan.
"That's all right," said Ted.
"For a little extra,
we will rent you a pair."

Stan ran home to get
the rest of his money.

·2·
PRACTICE

That afternoon a crowd went to the big
barn for the first lesson. They lined up,
wearing their rented tap shoes.

"Ready?" said Tonya.

"Music, please, Ted!"

Ted started the music.

"Everybody take one

step forward!"

said Tonya.

They all took

one step forward.

"Very good!" said Tonya. "Now one step back!"

Maureen stepped back onto Victor's foot.

Victor knocked over Myrtle,

Myrtle crashed into Grace,

Grace fell on Henry,

Henry landed on Dorothy,

and Dorothy stumbled over Stan.

"You'll have to do
better than that,
people,"
said Tonya.
"Or you can't be
in the big show."

"Give us another chance!" said Stan.
"Start again!" said Tonya. "Music, Ted!"

·3·
GETTING READY

Every night that week Mud Flat echoed
with the sound of practicing for the big show.

Stan worked especially hard.

Finally he fell asleep with his tap shoes on and dreamed of large crowds clapping.

But at rehearsals in the barn Stan couldn't seem
to get it right.

"No! No!" said Tonya. "Try it again—
hop, scuff, shuffle, hop!"

"Scuffle . . . hopple . . .
shlopple?" said Stan.
"Hoffle . . . shloffle . . . scup?"

Finally Tonya said, "Forget dancing in the big show,
Stan. You can put up the posters, sell tickets,
and make lemonade."

Stan went outside
and headed slowly
for home.
"Nobody ever claps
for lemonade,"
he said.

·4·

THE DAY BEFORE

Stan put up posters all over Mud Flat.

He sold tickets door to door.

"Would you like to buy
a ticket to the show,
Mrs. Reynolds?"

"I'll take
two,
please,
Stan."

Mr. Cusspid came by in his old car.
"Want to buy some tickets
to the big show,
Mr. Cusspid?"

"Are you crazy?" said Mr. Cusspid. "Pay good
money to watch a bunch of nincompoops make
fools of themselves?"
"There's going to be lemonade," said Stan.
"I hate lemonade," said Mr. Cusspid, and drove away,
honking his horn at everybody.

Stan sold the last tickets to Edna and Barry,
and turned in the money to Ted.

Pauline, who ran the fruit store,
gave Stan lots of free lemons.
"Thank you," said Stan.
"I like to give something to the village,"
said Pauline, "even if it's only lemons."

Stan squeezed all afternoon.
" . . . 312 . . . 313 . . . ," he counted.

Then Neddy came by. "Let me help," he said.

SQWOOSH!

LEMONS

In no time, all the lemons were squeezed,
and there was plenty of lemonade for everybody.

BAD NEWS

The next morning everybody in the show
turned up promptly for the last rehearsal.
But the van was gone.

"Where are Tonya and Ted?" said Maureen.

"Tonya and Ted drove away
in the middle of the night,"
said Eugene.

"Are they coming back?" said Sarah.

"I doubt it," said Eugene. "They kind of sneaked
out of here."

"What about the show?" said Benjamin.

"We've been rehearsing all week," said Clarissa.

"I sold all the tickets," said Stan.

"We made lots of lemonade,"
said Neddy.

"Never trust strangers,"
said Cynthia.

"I could have told you that!"

"Then why didn't you?"
said Warren.

Pretty soon everybody was arguing.

Stan and Maureen left.
"I guess I'd better take those posters down,"
said Stan.

"I guess you
should,"
said Maureen.
"I'll help you."

"That's the end of that,"
said Maureen.
"Wait a second,"
said Stan. "I have an idea."

An hour later Stan and Maureen
were putting up new signs.

·6·
THE ESCAPE

Far away, Tonya and Ted were driving through
the night. Tonya was looking at a map.
"Where shall we go next?" she said.

"I don't know," said Ted. "It's going to be
tough to find a town as dumb as Mud Flat."
"They were pushovers," said Tonya. "So trusting!"
"That's right," said Ted. "No fun at all."
"Well, we pulled it off, and it's over,"
said Tonya. "Forget about it."
They drove on in silence.

.7.

THE SHOW

At eight o'clock Stan stood on the stage of the
old barn and said, "Welcome, ladies and gentlemen,
to the Anyhow Show!"

The audience clapped.
"Oh, I like that," said Stan to himself.
When the clapping stopped, Stan said,
"How about that lemonade, folks?"
They all clapped again.

"Start the show, Stan!" yelled DeWitt.

Augie began to play the piano.

Neddy did an acrobatic tap.

Then Charlene and Kevin did a tango.

Deedee and Dolly performed a slithery
soft-shoe dance.

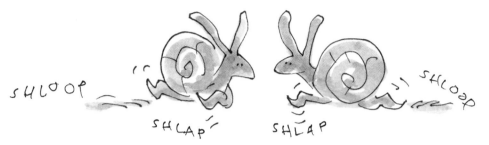

Nicholas danced on the
keys of the piano while
Marshall danced
on the pedals.

Maureen tapped very fast and gave a graceful bow.

Albert and Esther hauled a tub of water
onto the stage.
There was a moment of silence, and then . . .

Out of the water came Alex and Elise!

They did a water ballet.

The audience cheered.

Meanwhile, Mr. Cusspid was driving into his garage.
"Will you listen to those bozos down at that stupid
show?" he said.

Just then his car began to smoke
and rattle and shake.
"Probably needs a little oil,"
said Mr. Cusspid. He poured oil
into the engine, but most of it went
right through and onto the floor.

The car began to slide across the oily floor
and out of the garage.

The next thing Mr. Cusspid knew,
he was going down the hill.

"And for our next act," said Stan,

"we proudly present— What's that noise?"

Mr. Cusspid came flying through the air
and landed on the stage.

He tried to get up, but his shoes were too oily.

The crowd began to chant and dance
in time to the engine of Mr. Cusspid's car.

"Let's hear it for Mr. Cusspid!" said Stan,
as he slid him off the stage.

"Well, that's our show, ladies and gentlemen,"
said Stan. "Thank you all for coming.
There will be more lemonade—"

"Wait!" said a voice from offstage.

Tonya and Ted came tapping onto the stage!

"We changed our minds about leaving," said Ted.

"You were all such nice people."

"We'll be giving free lessons all this week," said Tonya.

"And you can keep your tap shoes, too!"

.8.
ANYHOW

"Great show, Stan!" said Maureen
when it was over.
"What's next year's going to be?"
said Augie.
"Bigger," said Stan, "and better!"
When Stan got home,
he put on his tap shoes.
"Maybe next year, I'll do a little
dance myself," he said. "It could
be a baseball number. . . ."

"I throw the ball
   in the air . . .

RAT-TA-TA
TAPITA   TAPITA
       TAP

"I do a quick tap dance, and . . .

"I catch the ball!"

SHUFFLE   SCUFFLE   SHUFF

"There's plenty of time to practice," he said.
He looked out the window at the moon
rising over Mud Flat and went to bed.